THE LITTLE BLACK BEAR WHO COULD NOT SLEEP

BY **ROBERT JENKINS**
ILLUSTRATED BY GAIL STORM

Printed in the United States of America

Illustrations by Gail Storm
Book layout by Claire Flint Last

Luminare Press
442 Charnelton St.
Eugene, OR 97401
www.luminarepress.com

LCCN: 2020908656
ISBN: 978-1-64388-394-6

Dr. Susan H.'s life has been intersected, by God, through personal, ministry, and professional roads at the global orphan crossroads. Personally, God led Susan and her family to adopt eight more children, ages seven to fourteen. From a ministry perspective (Hope at Home), God's call is to speak His hope of changing the world by transforming every orphan and vulnerable child into a beloved son or daughter. Professionally, Susan has worked in North America, South America, Eastern Europe, Asia, and Africa; she is a highly published scientist and is a senior advisor for global health at the Centers for Disease Control and Prevention. She is dedicated to using the best of science to forge broad governmental, civil society, and private partnerships that protect children and young people from violence and its enduring consequences.

Winter had come to the mountain.
Snow lay heavy and deep.
Bears hunkered down in their hideouts.
Cozy, snug, and asleep.

All except for
a little black bear named Boris...

Once upon a time, there was a little black bear. His name was Boris.

Boris was born in the mountains.
He was born in a cozy little cave.
Like all bears, Boris was born in winter.

For the first months of his life, Boris stayed snug asleep in his den with his mother.

They slept during the night. They slept during the day. They slept and they slept—all winter long.

In fact, it was not until early springtime that Boris's mother awakened her cub and led him out of the cave.

How exciting! There was warm sunshine and blue sky during the day. There were bright stars and moonlight at night. There were tall trees and green grass. There were rushing rivers and lovely lakes. High up, snow still covered the slopes. But as time passed, even the mountaintop meadows turned green.

Summer followed spring, and Boris grew bigger. His mother showed him where to find berries and nuts and how to catch fish in the streams. She taught him to recognize deer and elk and moose.

Then she explained to him that although bears had few enemies, there was one animal that could be very dangerous. That animal was called "two-legs."

"What does a two-leg look like?" asked Boris.

"You will see one soon enough," answered his mother.

How right she was. For the very next evening, Boris and his mother smelled something good. They followed their noses to a campground where people were barbecuing. "Those are the dangerous animals I warned you about," said mother bear.

Boris watched the group of two-legs. They were circled around a brightly burning fire. Boris had never seen fire. It frightened him.

"Two-legs sometimes leave food," said his mother. "But it is best to stay away when they are around. They have guns."

"What are guns?" asked Boris.

"Guns are big sticks that make a loud noise and kill elk and deer. When you hear the big boom of the guns, run and hide!"

Summer turned to autumn. The weather grew cold. And then, the snow came. First it fell in gentle flakes that melted. Then it came down harder and stayed on the ground. His mother said soon the snow would be like a deep blanket everywhere. It was time to return to their den.

"We will go home for a long, long sleep," said Mother.

"But I don't want to go back and sleep," said Boris. "I want to see the snow. I want to play in it. I want to see what happens in winter."

"Bears sleep during winter," said his mother.

"But why?" asked Boris.

"Because," said his mother.

"Because why?" asked Boris.

"Because that is just the way it is!" said his mother.

Reluctantly, Boris followed his mother back up the mountain. He paused outside the cave and looked back down the slope. He did not want to sleep. He wanted to explore. He did not want to go into the cave. He wanted to climb trees and catch fish. Most of all, he wanted to see what it was like in winter.

"Come," growled his mother impatiently. "It is time to settle down for winter."

So, into the cave they went.
They curled up and fell asleep.

Then one day, Boris woke up. It was dark in the den. His mother was sound asleep. But Boris was restless. "Maybe it's time to go out," he thought. "I will take a look."

And so Boris went to the entrance of the cave and poked his head outside. And when he did, he saw the most amazing sight. The sun blazed in a bright blue sky. A glistening white blanket covered the mountain. Icicles hung from the cave entrance and sparkled in the light. And when a breeze shook the snow from the trees, it fell like diamond dust to the ground.

"Winter!" thought Boris. "I will go and explore." Boris took his first step outside the den and immediately sank deep into the snow—up to his shoulders.

"Oh boy, what fun!" thought Boris.

He took a second step, brushing aside the deep powder with his strong legs, and then a third. Slowly, he managed to make his way down the mountain. Soon he became so confident that he began to run. But when he did, he tripped over a snow-covered log and tumbled head first down the slope.

Down,

    down,

       down

          he rolled

             like a

                big ball

                   of snow.

Faster and faster he went until suddenly—
bump!—he banged into a pine tree and came
to a halt. Ouch!

Boris brushed the snow from his eyes. And when
he did, he found himself nose to nose with...
a bighorn sheep.

"Who are you?" asked the sheep.

"I'm Boris."

"You are a little bear," said the sheep.
"You should be asleep in your den."

"I wanted to see winter," said Boris.
"Isn't it beautiful?!"

"Winter can be beautiful," said the sheep.
"But it can also be harsh. You should
go back to your den."

"I will," said Boris.
"But first I am going to explore."

The bighorn sheep shook his head and ambled off
through the snow. "You'll be sorry," he bleated
and then disappeared behind a snowdrift.

Boris paid no attention. He scampered farther down
the mountain. He became good at sliding down the
slope. And when he got to the top of a steep snowy
meadow, he decided to slide down the glade as far
and as fast as he could.

Wheee! Down, down he went. Faster and faster he slid. A lake appeared below, and Boris was heading right for it. But the little black bear couldn't stop! So, on he went until he slid out onto the lake. <u>Onto</u> the lake!

When he finally spun to a halt, Boris got back on all four legs. He stood on the ice of the frozen water. "I am standing on water!" giggled Boris. "How wonderful!"

Boris looked at the ice. He saw a fish move below. He reached out to grab it and banged his paw on the frozen surface. Ow! "It sure is hard to fish during the winter," he said to himself.

Boris headed back to the bank of the lake. But with each step his legs slipped out from under him and down he went onto the cold hard ice. He slipped and fell on his side. Ahh! He slipped and fell on his rump. Oooh!! He slipped and fell face first on his chin. Ouch!!!

Slowly slipping and sliding, Boris fumbled his way to the edge of the lake. He climbed up onto the bank. And when he lifted his head, he was staring up into the face of... an elk.

"Who are you?" asked the elk.

"I'm Boris."

"You are a little bear," said the elk. "You should be asleep in your den."

"I will," said Boris. "But first I want to explore."

The elk shook his head and ambled on up the mountain. "You'll be sorry," said the elk.

Boris paid no attention. Back in the snow, he walked into the woods and farther down the mountain.

His paw was bruised. His chin was sore. But Boris pressed on. He walked and he walked. And then he walked some more. The snow was deep, and the woods seemed endless. He could not remember the forest being so big in summer. Perhaps he had not visited this part of the mountain. Finally, the trees ended, and Boris came out onto a wide snow-covered slope.

But this slope was different. The snow was not fluffy and deep. It was hard and smooth. Boris was about to step onto the broad trail when all of a sudden—Whoosh! Something big swished by him. Then another—and another. Three animals slid down the mountain. They were two-legs! But these two-legged creatures were different. Their feet ended in long planks of wood that carried them downhill faster than Boris could imagine. Faster than a bear. Faster than a deer. Even faster than a mountain lion. Boris watched in wonder. Little did Boris know that he had stumbled into a ski resort.

The sun was setting. The temperature was dropping. For the first time, Boris felt a chill. But then he caught a whiff of something good. It was the smell he remembered from that night he first saw the two-legs. It was the smell of roasting meat. Suddenly Boris was hungry. Hungry and cold, the curious cub followed the scent down the mountain.

The smell led him to a house near the ski slope. Boris knew it must be the den of the two-legs. Smoke poured out of a tall stone chimney. And the good food smells swirled around him. Boris hesitated. His mother had told him to avoid the dangerous two-legged animals. But the smell was a powerful attraction. Boris moved closer. He went up to a large window, stood up on his hind legs, and looked in.

What a sight! The room was brightly lit. A fire blazed in the fireplace. But, most curious of all, centered in the window was a pine tree all decorated with lights and sparkling ornaments. Boris thought it splendid. It all looked warm and cozy. He thought of his own den and wished he were there.

The smell was coming from the other side of the house. Boris followed the scent until he came to the underside of a deck. The deck was supported by log columns. I can climb those, thought Boris. And sure enough, up he went until he got to the top. He clambered over the railing and onto the deck.

The kitchen looked onto the deck. Big glass doors stood between the bear and his supper.

Boris went up to the glass to look in. And when he did, he found himself face to face with... a little female two-legs.

The girl screamed. EEEK!

A mama two-legs appeared. She screamed. BEAR!!

Bright lights snapped on. More two-legs appeared. They shouted and shrieked. They banged pots and pans. Boris was scared stiff. The lights hurt his eyes. The noise hurt his ears. He scrambled back over the railing and started his climb down the column. Whoooah! Boris lost his grip. He half-slid, half-fell to the snow down below. He landed on his bottom—THUD! The two-legs rushed onto the deck, but by then Boris had disappeared into the darkness of the woods.

Boris scampered through the trees and headed up the mountain. His heart was pounding. His rump was sore. His chin still hurt. But he kept going and going until he could go no more. Tired of making his way uphill through the deep snow, Boris found a fallen tree that lay a few feet above ground. He crawled underneath to hide and to rest. He fell asleep.

Boris awoke to a dull light. It was snowing. Big flakes came down. A foot of fresh white powder had fallen during the night. The entrance to his little den was almost blocked up. Boris knocked the snow aside with his paw and crawled out of his hideaway.

"I want to go home," cried Boris. And so he started back up the mountain. The snow kept falling. The wind began blowing. Boris had trouble seeing. His tracks were covered over, and he could not remember his way. Up, up he trudged, hoping to find his trail. He was cold, and he was frightened.

"I wish I had listened to Mama," he thought. "I wish I had never left my warm, cozy cave."

After a long while, Boris came out of the woods onto a wide expanse of snow. He stepped out and immediately slipped and fell on his chin. Thump! "It's the lake!" shouted Boris.

And indeed it was, although the ice was now knee-deep in snow. Boris turned toward the bank and began to climb up a steep snowy meadow—the same one that he had tumbled down the day before. And when he got to the top, he found himself face to face with... a moose.

"Who are you?" asked the moose.

"I am Boris."

"You are a little bear," said the moose. "You should be asleep in your den."

"You are right," said Boris.

"You best get home then," said the moose.

"I am on my way," replied Boris.

And so, slowly but surely our little black bear made his way up the mountain and back to his cave. He had trouble finding it, as it was almost completely buried in snow. But finally, he saw a crack in the opening and crawled into his den. He lay down. He ached all over. He was cold, and he was tired. He snuggled up to his mother. But his movement and cold fur awakened her.

"Is it time to get up?" she said half asleep.

"No Mama, it's still winter."

"Would you like to go out and explore?"
she asked him.

"No thank you, Mother. I am a little bear.
I should be in my den in the winter,
and that is where I shall stay."

"What a good little bear," she said.

"Good night, Boris."

"Good night, Mama."

And good night to curious cubs—everywhere.

So, Boris crept back to his cave,
A colder but wiser bear.
And slept the rest of the winter
All snug in his cozy lair.

But sleep brought dreams of adventure—
Of wading through snow knee-deep,
Of a splendid indoor pine tree,
Of moose and a bighorn sheep.

He dreamt that he slid down the slopes,
Walked on frozen lakes and more.
And planned in his mind the next time
He might venture out to explore.

ROBERT JENKINS divides his time between the big cities of Europe and the Rocky Mountains of Montana. The story of Boris was inspired by wildlife encounters in Big Sky country.

An uninvited visitor climbs up
onto the author's deck...

Was it Boris or his mother?

CPSIA information can be obtained
at www.ICGtesting.com
Printed in the USA
BVHW021317230221
600892BV00008B/124